Put Beginning Readers on the Right Track with
ALL ABOARD READING™

The All Aboard Reading series is especially for beginning readers. Written by noted authors and illustrated in full color, these are books that children really and truly *want* to read—books to excite their imagination, tickle their funny bone, expand their interests, and support their feelings. With three different reading levels, All Aboard Reading lets you choose which books are most appropriate for your children and their growing abilities.

Level 1—for Preschool through First Grade Children
Level 1 books have very few lines per page, very large type, easy words, lots of repetition, and pictures with visual "cues" to help children figure out the words on the page.

Level 2—for First Grade to Third Grade Children
Level 2 books are printed in slightly smaller type than Level 1 books. The stories are more complex, but there is still lots of repetition in the text and many pictures. The sentences are quite simple and are broken up into short lines to make reading easier.

Level 3—for Second Grade through Third Grade Children
Level 3 books have considerably longer texts, use harder words and more complicated sentences.

All Aboard for happy reading!

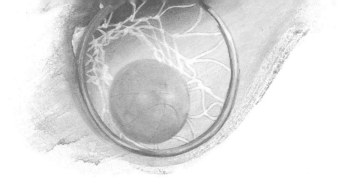

For my father—S.A.K.

To my wife Sandy and children
Melanie, Timothy, Danny—M.H.

Special thanks to Wayne Patterson, Naismith Memorial Basketball Hall
of Fame.

Photo credits: p. 15, Fernando Medina/NBA Photos; p. 27, Rocky Widner/NBA Photos; p. 31
and back cover, Andrew Bernstein/NBA Photos; p. 47, Layne Murdoch/NBA Photos.

Library of Congress Cataloging-in-Publication Data

Kramer, Sydelle.
  Hoop stars / by S.A. Kramer ; illustrated by Mitchell Heinze.
    p.   cm.—(All aboard reading)
  "Level 3, grades 2-3."
  Summary: Describes the lives of noted basketball players David Robinson, Charles Barkley,
Hakeem Olajuwon, and Shaquille O'Neal.
  1. Basketball players—United States—Biography—Juvenile literature. [1. Basketball
players.] I. Heinze, Mitchell, ill. II. Title. III. Series.
GV884.A1K73   1995
796.323′092′2—dc20
  [B]
                                                                        95-4993
                                                                          CIP
ISBN 0-448-40944-5 (GB)   B C D E F G H I J   AC

ISBN 0-448-40943-7 (pbk)   B C D E F G H I J

ALL
ABOARD
READING™

Level 3
Grades 2-3

HOOP STARS

By S. A. Kramer
Illustrated by Mitchell Heinze

With photographs

Grosset & Dunlap • New York

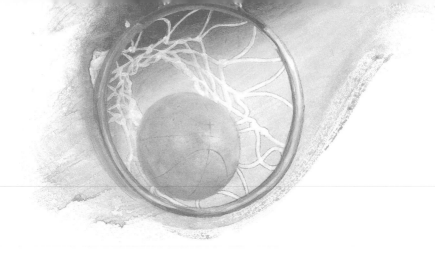

Rocket Man

Africa, 1979. A dusty soccer field in a country called Nigeria. Hakeem Olajuwon (You say it like this: uh-LI-juh-wan.) is leaning against the goal. He's got his eye on a stranger who has been watching his every move. Hakeem can't help wondering why the man is there.

Hakeem is a sixteen-year-old who belongs to a tribe called the Yoruba. (You say it like this: YOR-uh-buh.) Most Yorubas are farmers, but Hakeem's

father is a businessman. His family has lived in the city for years.

Olajuwon means "always on top" in the Yoruba language. It's a good name for Hakeem, since he's already six-foot-eight. A terrific athlete, he loves soccer and a sport called team handball.

Hakeem is surprised when the stranger suddenly walks up to him. It

turns out he's a basketball coach looking for new players. He says Hakeem can be a basketball star.

Basketball? Hakeem has never played it. In Africa it's a new sport. Only a few athletes know the rules. Most Africans have never even seen a game.

Still, Hakeem agrees to try. Soon it's clear the coach is right. Hakeem is very talented. He makes Nigeria's best team in just a few months.

But he finds it's not easy to play basketball in his country. There aren't many courts. There's only one big indoor arena. Hakeem can't even find

sneakers to fit his size 16 feet. He ends up playing in a pair too small for him.

One day an American sees him on the court. He feels Hakeem can become a great center. So he sets up a tryout for him. It is at the University of Houston in Texas. If Hakeem makes the team, he'll go to college for free.

At the tryout the coach feels Hakeem is too skinny. And too polite. Players can push him around on the court. But Hakeem is quick, and he jumps very high. His feet leave the floor so fast he's like a rocket taking off. The coach decides to take a chance. Hakeem makes the team.

At first he is thrilled. Then he is homesick. More than thirty thousand students go to the university. Hakeem doesn't know a single one. He's so shy he's afraid to talk.

Hakeem doesn't fit in. He wears an African robe called a dashiki. (You say it like this: da-SHEE-kee.) He bows whenever he meets someone. People spell his name Akeem, but he doesn't tell them they're wrong.

Hakeem isn't even sure what to eat.

He's never had a salad or fried chicken.
American food seems so strange, he eats
only oysters and biscuits. They remind
him of home.

He feels lost on the court, too. His teammates understand the game better. They are more fit. After playing for just five minutes, Hakeem is worn out. Although he's now six-foot-ten, he can't slam-dunk.

But Hakeem learns the rules. He listens carefully and picks up the names of all the plays. To gain some weight, he starts eating steak and vanilla ice cream.

As he gets stronger, he starts to play tough. With his long arms and quick jump, he blocks a lot of shots. It's hard to keep him away from the basket. Soon he's the most feared college player of his time.

In 1984 the Houston Rockets sign him to play in the NBA. Nicknamed "The Dream," he never stops practicing. He shoots 500 jump shots every day.

Hakeem becomes a leading rebounder and scorer. In 1989 he sets a record. He's the first player to block over 200 shots and to make over 200 steals.

The next year, he becomes the third NBA player ever to make a "quadruple double." That means he scored 10 or more points, pulled down 10 or more rebounds, passed for 10 or more assists, and blocked 10 or more shots—all in one game!

Today most experts feel Hakeem is basketball's best center. In 1992–93 he won the NBA Defensive Player of the Year Award. In 1993–94 he was named MVP (Most Valuable Player).

It's hard to believe he was once a skinny teenager who had never been on a basketball court. Now he's one of the game's true superstars.

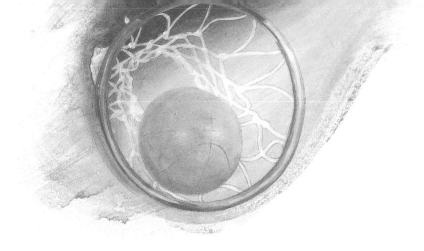

The Volcano

January 18, 1993. The New York Knicks are beating the Phoenix Suns, 106–103. Only twelve seconds are left in the close game. Suddenly Charles Barkley, the Suns' star forward, gets the ball. Everyone knows Charles hates to lose.

From 3-point range, he fires one last shot. A miss! But Charles is sure he was fouled. He can't believe it when the referee doesn't make the call.

The Suns are beaten. Charles is mad. He's well-known for his temper tantrums. He kicks chairs and shakes tables. If people boo, he may throw Gatorade or spit at them. He screams at fans—once he even hit one.

As the referee leaves the court, Charles shouts at him. He blames the man for the Suns' loss. A teammate tries

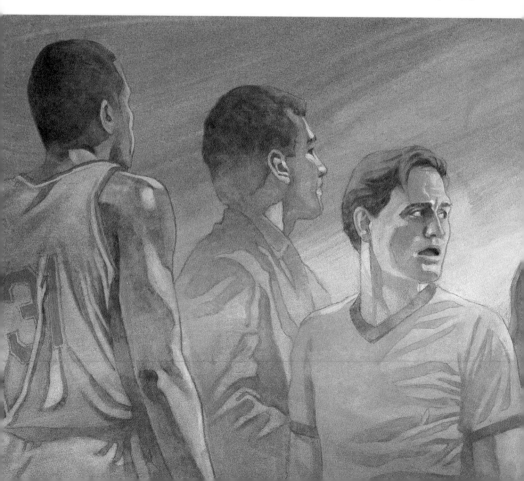

to quiet him—arguing with refs is against the rules. If Charles doesn't stop, he might have to pay a fine. He may even have to sit out games.

But Charles just keeps yelling. He seems angry enough to punch someone. Suddenly he charges toward the ref. The fans can't believe it. Nobody ever does that!

The ref takes off down the runway to the locker rooms. He's trying to get away. Charles rushes after him—but the scorers' table blocks his path.

The table is piled high with computers. Charles easily springs over it. He may be only six-foot-five, but he outjumps taller men. In games he has leapt 39 inches into the air.

Charles hurls himself down the runway. He's still hollering after the ref. But the man has disappeared—the chase is over.

Charles knows his temper has landed him in trouble again.

Later he is fined ten thousand dollars. He must also sit out one game. When he is calmer, he admits, "I made a mistake."

Many people describe Charles as a

human volcano. He plays hard all the time, and gets mad at those who don't. Some fans say he's a show-off with a big mouth. Others feel he only says what he thinks.

But everyone agrees he's a great scorer and rebounder. He's come a long way from his childhood in a poor section of Alabama.

When Charles was a teenager, he stole for the fun of it. But one night the police almost caught him. After that, he swore not to waste his life. He hoped playing basketball might save him.

Yet the game was hard for Charles to learn. At first he couldn't even make his high school team.

So Charles practiced every night. At the playground, he shot hoop after hoop. To learn to jump, he leapt a 4-foot fence over and over. He wouldn't give up.

By the time he went to Auburn University, Charles had become a good player. He had quick moves and sure hands, and he never took his eyes off the ball. Although he was overweight, he was known for his great defense. He was nicknamed the Round Mound of Rebound.

In 1984, he began his NBA career. As a member of the Philadelphia 76ers, he learned how to score. He taught himself a jump shot and how to leap toward the basket. Now he can twist his body into amazing positions in the air. With his combination of strength and speed, he's one of the NBA's leading scorers and rebounders. He's been an All-Star every year since 1987.

Despite his temper, Charles is popular with the fans. They know how much he loves the game. Even when he's badly injured, it's hard to keep him off the court.

Charles may be the shortest forward in the NBA, but many feel he's the best. Known as "Sir Charles," he was voted MVP in 1992-93. He's one player who made his teenage dreams come true.

Now he has an even greater dream— to run for office, and help his country. Knowing Charles, he'll be tough to beat.

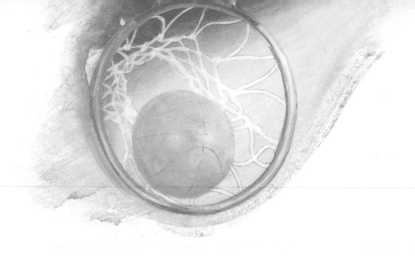

Shaq Attack

August 7, 1992. The Orlando Arena in Florida. Dozens of reporters jam a big room downstairs. TV cameras are rolling. Flashbulbs are popping. All eyes are on one man, who stands head and shoulders above the crowd. He's twenty-year-old Shaquille O'Neal.

Only a few weeks ago, Shaq was one of the best college basketball players in the country. Now he's leaving his school, Louisiana State University, early. He's just signed a contract with the NBA's Orlando Magic. The Magic will

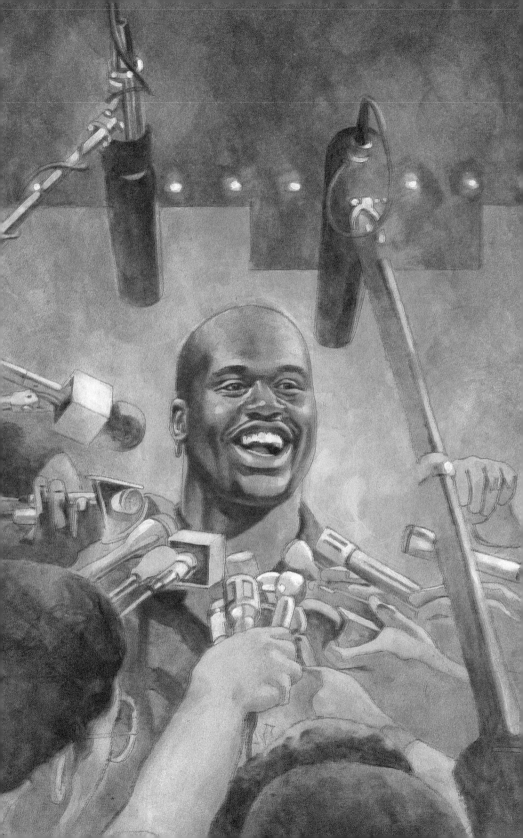

pay him more than any rookie has ever earned—forty-one million dollars for seven seasons.

Shaq has made it to the top faster than any basketball player before him. He's an NBA star without even scoring a point. That's because most teams don't have a player so gigantic.

Shaq's name means "little one," but he's a mountain of a man. He's seven-foot-one and weighs over 300 pounds. Even his feet are huge—he wears size 21 shoes. He can lift 250 pounds in weights.

Quick and strong, Shaq's exciting to watch on the court. He rams through the other team to get to the hoop. The arena seems to shake whenever he slam-dunks.

But Shaq is a gentle giant. One friend calls him a cross between Bambi and the Terminator. He's warm and friendly. People like to be around him. Already popular with the fans, he's been asked to make TV commercials, movies, and rap records.

Some experts feel he could be the greatest center ever. Others worry that people expect too much of him. They say NBA basketball is much tougher

than the college game. They're not sure
Shaq will seem so good when he's up
against the best.

Shaq knows he has to prove himself.
He feels he's not a great player yet. After
all, he hasn't been serious about
basketball for long. His father taught
him the game when he was seven, but
for years he wanted to be a dancer. In
school his teachers would complain
because he break-danced in the halls.

Just a few years ago, Shaq felt embarrassed by his height. By the age of thirteen, he was six-foot-eight. Other kids thought he was dumb because he was so big. They made fun of his size, so he hunched over to seem smaller. All Shaq wanted was "to be normal." Basketball made him feel better about himself.

Now he's part of the NBA.

In his first few games he works hard to show his talent. Quickly he becomes a scoring leader. But some fans aren't happy with him. At times he doesn't seem to understand the game. He often loses the ball and misses foul shots. There are people who say he's not a truly powerful player.

Then on April 23, 1993, Shaq proves them wrong. The Magic are playing the

New Jersey Nets. Right near the basket, Shaq snatches a pass. He springs high in the air and slam-dunks the ball hard.

As he dunks, he grabs the rim of the hoop. Hanging in the air, he bends his legs as if he's in a chair.

Suddenly something snaps. The basket slowly topples over. Down come the glass backboard and the 24-second clock. The whole goal is falling to the ground.

Shaq leaps off. He tries to get out of the way. The clock smacks him on the head, but he calmly walks off the court.

Players on both benches leap to their feet. The twenty thousand fans in the arena stand in shock. Other players have shattered glass backboards. But Shaq is the first player ever to have broken the goal.

He didn't mean to do it—but his dunk has cracked steel! It's no wonder he has a Superman tattoo on his left arm. No one questions his strength anymore. Shaq's the most powerful man in the game.

At the end of the season, he's named Rookie of the Year. His 322 slam dunks are an NBA record. He's the only player to finish in the top ten in points, rebounds, blocks, and shooting percentage.

The next year, he's even better. He's first in shooting percentage, second in scoring and rebounds, and sixth in blocked shots. In his third season, he becomes the league's leading scorer.

It's been a long time since Shaq wished he wasn't so tall.

Whiz Kid

San Antonio, Texas. November 4, 1989. David Robinson is nervous. He's the new center for the San Antonio Spurs. And this is his very first NBA game.

The fans have been waiting a long time for David. The team signed him up in 1987, but he couldn't play. First he had to serve two years in the navy. Now he's starting a new life.

The Spurs haven't had a winning season for seven years. David knows the fans are counting on him to change that.

Seven-foot-one, David's one of the fastest centers ever. Since he's left-handed, he's hard to guard. He's thin as a board, but his arms bulge with muscles. His sense of balance is so good he can walk on his hands across the court.

But David has always wondered if he
wants basketball to be his career. "I
never dreamed," he says, "of being a pro
in any sport." Basketball is just one of
many things he likes.

Serious and smart, David learned to
read when he was three. A math whiz,
he took college computer courses at
fourteen. He loved music so much that
he would practice the piano for hours.

He was a good athlete. But he never let sports take over his life. He didn't even play for his high school basketball team until his senior year.

Since David's father was in the navy, he wanted to join, too. He decided to go to college at the Naval Academy. He'd learn to be an engineer—and play basketball for fun.

But suddenly David grew five more inches. Now he was too tall to serve inside a ship, plane, or submarine. Yet his new height helped him to be a better player. He became a college hoop star in just a year.

But no matter how good he was, he never seemed to go all out in a game. On the court, his mind would wander. He later said, "I was lazy." He enjoyed basketball, but he wasn't sure he wanted it to be his job.

Now, in his first NBA game, he'll find out if he truly loves the sport. Can he become the great center the fans expect? All eyes are on him as he gets ready to play. The Spurs face one of the best teams in the country. Magic Johnson's Los Angeles Lakers.

During the game, David seems relaxed. He makes good shots and grabs a lot of rebounds. But he's secretly tense—so tense that he throws up at halftime. Whenever he's on the bench, he jiggles his knee madly. At least, he thinks, the Spurs have the lead.

Then late in the third quarter, the Lakers score 9 points in a row. Now the Spurs are ahead by only a basket. Magic gets the ball and drives in for a layup. The game seems sure to be tied.

But David is guarding the basket. He leaps into the air. With his powerful long arms, he hammers the shot away. Blocked! The Lakers don't score. David's made the game's most important play.

The Spurs go on to win 106–98. David finishes with 23 points and 17 rebounds. He's had a first game any rookie would be proud of.

The rest of David's season is just as great. He is named Rookie of the Year.

He gets better and better. In 1993–94 he becomes the fourth player in history to get a quadruple double. In 1994–95 he is named MVP.

Today David never wonders how much he wants to play pro basketball. He's out on the court with everything he's got. He says, "Basketball is my chance to be great."